W9-BZO-063

SCOOBY-DOO!

THE CAMPING CAPER

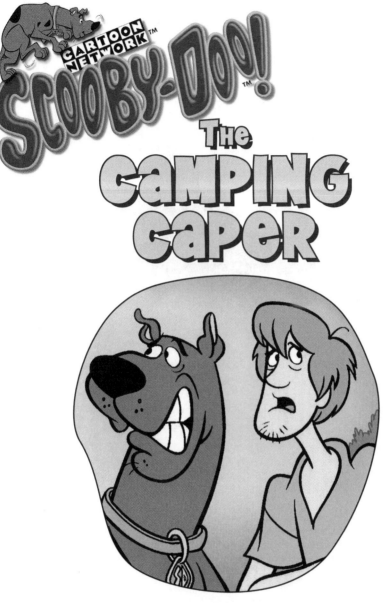

By Gail Herman
Illustrated by Duendes del Sur

SCHOLASTIC INC.
New York Toronto London Auckland Sydney
Mexico City New Delhi Hong Kong Buenos Aires

ISBN 0-439-80942-8

12 11 10 9 8 7 6 5 4   9 10/0

Designed by Michael Massen
Printed in the U.S.A.
First printing, January 2006

"It was a dark and spooky night," Velma spoke in a low voice. "Five friends gathered around a campfire in the woods. When suddenly—"

"Like, hold on there, Velma!" Shaggy jumped to his feet. He looked at the gang: Velma, Daphne, Fred, and Scooby-Doo.

They were camping out in Coolsville Woods. The sun was setting. A chilly wind was blowing. And Shaggy decided he didn't want to hear a scary story.

"Uh . . . uh . . . ," he stammered.
"Like, the fire is going out. We need
more firewood. Right, Scoob?"
"Right, Raggy!"

"Good idea, guys," said Daphne. "You should take a flashlight."

"Yeah," said Fred. "It's starting to get dark."

7

Shaggy grabbed a few slices of bread, too. "Think I'll do a Hansel and Gretel," he whispered to Scooby. "Leave a trail so we can find our way back."

Shaggy and Scooby set off. Shaggy broke off bits of bread. He dropped them on the ground. "Like, Scoob, good buddy, how do you find firewood, anyway?" Shaggy asked.

In the darkness, Scooby shrugged.
"I can barely see you," Shaggy said,
sounding a little scared.

Quickly, Shaggy picked a stick up off the ground. "Think this is enough?"
Scooby nodded. "Ruh huh!"
"Let's follow those bread crumbs!" Shaggy said.

They turned around.
The bread crumbs were gone!
"Scooby!" Shaggy cried. "You ate the bread."
Scooby shook his head. "Ro way. Rot me!"
"Dog's honor?" asked Shaggy.
"Rog's ronor," Scooby repeated.

Whooooo! Whoooo!

A moaning noise filled the woods. A shadow flitted over their heads.

"A ghost!" Shaggy clutched Scooby. "A ghost ate the bread."

The friends stood rooted to the spot. But all was quiet.

"Man, that's crazy." Shaggy took a deep breath. "Ghosts don't eat!"

Crack! Twigs snapped in the distance. *CRACK!* Twigs snapped again, closer this time.

Something scrambled right past them.

Shaggy shone his flashlight. Bright yellow eyes stared back.

"Ahhhh!" Shaggy, yelled. The creature disappeared.

"So, there is one ghost," he said. "And there is one . . . ," Shaggy scratched his head, thinking. "Wolf?"

"Rarerolf?" asked Scooby. He turned his head, searching the woods.

"Werewolf?" Shaggy shouted. "You're right, Scoob! That werewolf ate the bread! And I bet it's coming for us next!"

Shaggy and Scooby ran. Finally, they stopped to catch their breath. They stood in a clearing circled by trees.

"It's quiet here," said Shaggy. "No strange sounds, no strange creatures." *THUD! THUD!* Heavy footsteps echoed all around.

"Zoinks!" cried Shaggy. "What can it be now? Ghosts don't have feet. And werewolves are really quiet."

All at once, something dropped on their heads.
"The trees!" shouted Shaggy. "The trees are
alive! They're making those sounds! They're
throwing things at us!"

C-r-r-k! Loud creaking noises came from every which way.

"More trees!" Shaggy trembled. "They're pulling up roots. They're coming from all over the woods!"

The ground shook. Strange voices floated through the air. Shaggy and Scooby held each other tight. They squeezed their eyes shut.

"Like, whatever happens, good buddy," said Shaggy, "we're in this together."

"Open your eyes," a voice commanded.
"That tree's voice?" Shaggy hissed to Scooby.
"It sounds just like . . . ," he opened one eye.

"Velma!" Shaggy cried. "What
are you guys doing here? Where
are the crazy trees? Where are the
werewolves? Where are the ghosts?"

"What are you talking about?" asked Daphne as they walked to the campsite.

"Well," said Shaggy, "first something flew by our heads making this weird noise."

"Rhost!" put in Scooby. "Right rhere!" He pointed a paw.

"That's no ghost," said Velma. "It's an owl."

"Then a werewolf with yellow eyes gobbled up all our bread crumbs!" Shaggy said.

"There's a raccoon chewing on some bread," said Velma. "That must be what ate your bread crumbs."

"But the trees came alive and were throwing things," Shaggy went on. *Bonk!* Something hit him on the head. "Like that!" he cried.

Velma picked up an acorn. "A squirrel must have thrown this!"

Shaggy sighed. "What about the loud footsteps? The creaking nosies? And the voices?"

"That was us," said Velma. "We were looking for you. We all took different paths. Our voices sounded strange in the woods. And the branches creaked when we pushed past them."

"Oh," Shaggy gulped. He held out the stick. "Here's the firewood."

"Not much good for a fire," said Daphne.

"But it's perfect for roasting marsh-mallows!" said Shaggy.

"Rarshrallows?" asked Scooby-Doo. "Rum, rum!"